Corridors

part BEFORE

romance thriller

BY

Valerii Titov

Cover design by Germancreative-fiverr
Book design by creationcentre-fiverr

ISBN 9781976772092

Printed in the United States of America

Dedication

I dedicate this book to my family in the form of my beloved wife Lilia, and my two sons Julian and Anton. My black cat, Zhuzha, was next to me while I wrote this part of the trilogy. I want to thank Raul Martin from 'the City of Gold', Johannesburg, South Africa, for his input as well.

Other books by Valerii Titov include CORRIDORS sister novels, STRONGHOLDS and X-Ray Days, as well as Gift (a story of a family dog, and ABC book Alphabet (active book colouring).

E-mail : valeriititov.sr@gmail.com

Twitter: @alanfalconX

amazon.com/author/valerii-titov

Valerii Titov

December   **2017**

Contents

Author's Note

University of Chicago final year planetology student Glory Carter is every guy's dream. Her goddess looks, sexy figure and brains to go with it, makes all the guys' heads turn, but she has yet to find the one and only true love.

Eventually, Cupid's Arrows strike and she nets an archaeologist, Adam Kennedy, but when he disappears during a top-secret trip to the Amazon, things startedgetting out of hand for Glory.

Soon, her life is up in the air in more ways than you can imagine and with Adam seemingly gone

I hope this Romance/Thriller will bring readers as much pleasure as it did to me when writing it.

Warning: If you start reading 'Corridor' by Valerii Titov, you won't want to stop reading!

Valerii Titov December 2017

Chapter One

The President's Relative, or not

"Glory, are you really the grand-daughter of former US President Jimmy Carter?" asked thenaïve, brunette Deborah Summers, as she sat opposite Glory Carter during lunch break in the canteen at the University of Chicago, Illinois.

Glory Carter, the 20-year-old final year planetology student, gripped the fork in her right hand even tighter.

"Do I look like a peanut to you, Debbie?" responded Glory, with reference to Jimmy Carter's days as a peanut farmer outside of his political career.

"For the hundredth time this year, I am not Jimmy Carter's grand-daughter, or even related to him."

Jennifer Ellis, who was seated next to Deborah, grinned with satisfaction. She wasn't the leader of the Glory Carter fan club. The feeling was mutual because Glory didn't like or trust Jennifer that much either. Fashion-conscious Jennifer, wearing the latest Levis jeans and Lipsy Cold Shoulder blouse that left very little still covered.

In Glory's mind, Jennifer Ellis was the poor little rich girl who got everything that she wanted in life. Few people would put up with Jennifer's bitchy attitude, so she had found a way to stick to Glory like a leach.

Jennifer decided to stir things up even more.

"So who are you going to the prom dance with, Glory?"

Glory sighed and pushed her black hair away from her face. She was dateless but not desperate. After all, with the facial figures and body she has been blessed with, almost every guy at the University of Chicago had tried to hit on her, but with no luck.

"Oh my gosh! Glory, you don't have a date! " Jennifer summarized.

Deborah Summers, a year younger than her two student colleagues, rallied to Glory's defence.

"Please Jen, Glory has got more guys texting her in a month than you have had in your lifetime."

Jennifer was a firm believer in the philosophy that 'two is a company and three is a crowd'.

"I did not ask for your opinion, Miss 'I suck up to the Professors'," retorted the red-haired Jennifer.

Jennifer, turned her attention back to Glory.

"I wasn't trying to be mean, Glory,"

"It's just that you are never seen with a guy and some people might think that you are, well…"

Glory's left hand took a firm grasp on her plastic cup. If Jennifer even suggested that some students thought that Glory was possibly lesbian, the student queen of glitz and glamour was about to have her expensive clothes covered in orange juice.

Jennifer spoke in the nick of time.

"What about that archaeology student, Adam Kennedy? He is always staring at you."

"Kennedy..." chipped in Deborah.

"Is he related to the late US President, JF Kennedy?"

Glory sniggered.

First, it was her surname in connection with Jimmy Carter and now, Adam Kennedy and the assassinated US leader of the 1960s.

"Well, if you don't want him, I will move in," Jennifer said with reference to the good-looking Adam.

"He is quite a catch."

Glory had to choose her words carefully. She had noticed 22-year-old Adam Kennedy and he had definitely noticed her. She was playing the hard-to-get game her mother had taught her.

"'Don't let any man think that you are easy, Glory." Robyn Carter had once told her daughter.

"Be my guest with Adam," Glory told her giving Deborah a side wink. Glory might only be 20 years old, but she was streetwise and knew that Jennifer's money and expensive clothes would not net a guy of Adam's calibre.

"All right then, Glory. I will leave you to keep on looking down your telescopic lens and maybe Mr Right will magically appear for you someday," Jennifer" said as she, Jennifer, rose from her seat and headed off with her lunch tray.

"That bitch,"Deborah remarked once Jennifer was out of earshot.

"You said it, I thought it," said Glory.

Adam Kennedy stood in conversation with a fellow male student at the far side of the canteen, but it was clear that he had his eyes firmly on Glory, but not for long though.

The moment he saw Jennifer Ellis actioning her sexy hip-moving walk towards him, he knew what was coming next and his sprint from the area would have made 2016 Olympic double gold medalist speedster.

Usain Bolt looks sluggish beside him

Glory and Deborah burst out laughing but hid their faces behind their university textbooks to avoid Jennifer seeing that they were laughing at her and not with her.

What Glory didn't know was that she was being watched by another interested party. Alan Falcon, 23, son of a billionaire pharmaceutical businessman, Rex Falcon. Healso has eyes for Glory and wanted her as his girl. Although, he knew that time was running out as the university year was about to end.

Both Adam and Alan had a common thought with regards to Glory prom night; it had to be prom night. Neither of them planned on asking Glory to accompany them to the prom. Both planned to make their move when they saw her at the function.

"So who are you really going with to prom night?" Deborah asked Glory again as the girls packed away their lunch trays.

Again Glory just sighed.

How she wished that for once in her tertiary life, she could say that she had a date for a major function. It seemed that true love and relationships were not for her. Goodness knows it was not for lack of trying on her part or the guys who had literally stalked her over the years.

University of Chicago gridiron football star, Bobby Bryant had dated her for a short period, but Glory had felt that she was being used more as a showpiece that he could show offto his friends at parties, rather than as a girlfriend.

Then, there was her short fling with the university's basketball point guard, Joe Green. Besides being a good two foot taller than her, he too seemed more interested in everything around him than a solid relationship.

Perhaps she was too choosy, she had often thought, but then why did her friends get it right and she couldn't make any headway when it came to relationships?

Some of her friends from her school days had already become mothers, some even before they had become brides. Glory wanted to go through the proper route. She wanted to be married before becoming a mother.

Even Planetology, Professor Jeff Conway, had attempted to take Glory away for a weekend to 'teach her more', but the black-haired student saw right through the professor's agenda and thought up an excuse to get out of that one.

She had begun to think that she would be single forever and in-fact, was starting to like the feeling. It meant less trouble in her life, but it brought with it a deep sense of loneliness.

"Well if it makes you feel any better, I haven't got a date for the prom either," blushed Deborah.

Glory smiled. Deborah does not have model looks like she had, but there was something about her that was attractive to men. Deborah was an innocent girl, who had joined the University of Chicago straight from a convent school. It had been quite a mind change for her, but fortunately, she had landed Glory as a friend.

Deborah put on her sunglasses and looked towards the sky.

"Glory, do you really believe that there is something out there?" she asked.

"You mean like men from the moon who will come to earth and sweep us off our feet?" teased Glory.

Deborah giggled.

"Something like that too, but I was actually asking if you believe that there are lifeforms on the other planets?"

"I believe that could well be the case," replied Glory.

"What about Unidentified Flying Objects," asked Deborah.

"You know what I mean. What about UFOs?'

Deborah just shrugged.

"I have never been to space, but some people who have been staring through telescopes longer than I have, have reported seeing some strange things floating around in the solar system."

Deborah pressed further on the matter.

"What about that Malaysian Airlines Flight number 370 that disappeared off the planet on 8 March 2014? Did it really disappear down the famous Black Hole in outer space or did some military force like the Russians, accidentally shoot it down?"

Glory shook her head. Even as a student of planetology, she did not buy into the fact that the aircraft with 227 people onboard, had been swallowed up by the Black Hole. Something earthly must have happened to it. While she was a Christian church-goer, she didn't believe in the supernatural elements. Her mind let her believe that there had to be a logical reason for something to happen.

Glory turned to her friend.

"At least we will have the most stunning dresses at the prom even if we are dateless," quipped Glory.

Deborah teased Glory.

"Guys drool over you no matter what you wear, so pick the guy that you want and pass one of your other contenders over to me."

"You went to school in Dallas, Texas, didn't you?" asked Glory.

Deborah nodded.

"Yeah, that is part of the problem as most of the honest guys I know live in that part of the world," she said.

Glory burst out laughing.

"So you really do believe that there is something such as an honest guy?" she questioned.

This time, it was Deborah's turn of to nod.

"I believe in that as much as you believe in life outside Planet Earth," remarked Deborah.

Deborah stopped walking which forced Glory to stop too.

"So what about Adam Kennedy?" asked Deborah.

"What about him?" queried Glory.

"Come on, Glory, I have been your friend for some time now and I know there is something in the air between both of you. I have seen the way you look at each other. It's like two teenagers who are refusing to make the first move. You had better move fast if you want to get him before someone else does."

Glory grinned.

"Was it that obvious?" she said.

"Glory, at prom night, you either go for it or else, well, you know, if you snooze you lose," advised Deborah.

Glory nodded intensely. Deborah was right. They were all going to leave the University of Chicago soon and the opportunity to get to know Adam Kennedy better might be lost. She wanted to live her life with no regrets. She needed to make something happen at prom night.

The girls bid each other farewell, but instead of returning to her student accommodation, Glory went to the Planetology laboratory where she had spent most of her time as a student.

She removed the lens cover on the Celestron CPC 1100 StarBright telescope and positioned her body behind it. Even though it was now around 13h30, the equipment was powerful enough to see much in the solar system.

As she zoomed the lens towards the planets that could be seen, a sharp light blinded her and she pulled away from the telescope.

Glory wiped her face and peered again through the telescope. The light ray that had stunned her was gone. Had she imagined it? It was almost like something out there was zooming in on Planet Earth? Without proof, it would be a hard story to sell to her professor.

Glory looked again and again but she couldn't see what it was again through the telescope. Was she going crazy? No, Glory, she thought, there is definitely something out there!

Glory Carter had lost track of time. Her main aim in life now was not finding a man but finding the light ray that had blinded her a short while earlier.

It was another hour and a half before another light ray tried to blind her through the telescope, but this time, it was not as powerful as the first one. It was almost as if the light rays were aimed directly at her telescope. In all her studies, she had never seen such solar system behaviour before.

It was like something or someone, many, many miles away was targeting something sinister against Planet Earth or Glory Carter!

Chapter Two

It's raining on Prom Night

The University of Chicago's famous Ratner Athletics Center is usually filled to its capacity for basketball matches involving the home team known as the 'Maroons'. This time, the hall had an even neater look about it as it played host to Prom Night 2017.

Not even an early evening downpour over Chicago could dampen the spirits of those in attendance as Local Organizing Committee members ushered guests into the main arena.

The venue was already pretty full by the time Glory Carter and Deborah Summers arrived. Was it Glory's imagination or did a sudden hush go over the arena as she stepped into it? Dressed in a pink Cliffon solid half sleeve ballroom gown, her beauty was simply too much for many in the room to handle. This applied none more so than to Professor Jeff Conway, who eyed Glory up and down, before getting a poke in the ribs from his wife, Minnie, who was standing next to him.

Deborah Summers, dressed in a blue A-line Princess van Eck floor length dress was now almost the same height as Glory, as she wore her Royer Vivier shoes. Many in the room thought that Glory was a bit of a loner. She rarely mixed with the other girls at parties. More to the point, and she rarely went to parties. Her strategy was to rather save her cash over a year so she could look the part at prom night.

At this point, Glory could not see Adam Kennedy in the arena. Over in the far corner, standing alone, was Alan Falcon, dressed in a Dolce and Gabbana black suit.

He wasn't alone for long.

"Hi, Alan," said Jennifer Ellis.

Alan did his best to escape but soon realized that he could not achieve his goal without causing a scene.

"Hello, Jennifer You look lovely tonight," he said more out of routine than compliment.

Glory and Deborah watched the goings-on from the far end. Glory immediately noticed that there was something wrong with Jennifer's outfit – a red strapless floor length gown.

There was way too much loose material around her waist area. Was Jennifer pregnant or fat or both? Or had she just got the measurements wrong when briefing the dress designer?

Something made Glory look towards the main entrance and there he was. Adam Kennedy had arrived, looking as handsome as ever in his grey Hugo Boss suit.

Glory couldn't help but notice that Adam had arrived alone and watched on as he made his way over to the bar where a student was acting as a barman, empowered him with a Bad Light beer – Alabama's finest.

Glory tried not to stare at Adam, but it was hard not to do that. Deborah nudged her friend so hard in the ribs that the black haired girl nearly fell over.

"Remember what you told me you were going to do tonight?" remarked Deborah.

Glory thought intensely about the situation.

"Alright, Debbie, I have got this under control. I just need the right time to do it."

Moving towards the bar now, was Alan with Jennifer Ellis a stride behind him.

She suddenly saw Adam and poor Alan was history, or lucky.

"Adam, you look even more handsome today," said Jennifer.

The archaeology student never reacted to the compliment as he had just noticed Glory on the other side of the room.

As pretty as Jennifer tried to be, she couldn't hold a candle to Glory Carter in terms of looks, sex appeal, and for that matter, personality.

Their gazes met each other and Adam tossed his head to one side as if to point towards a vacant table where they could meet.

Deborah pushed a glass of cola tonic, lemonade and ice into her friend's right hand and whispered: "You go, girl".

Seated on plastic chairs which were covered to match the room's red and white décor, it seemed another stalemate as both Adam and Glory waited for the other to speak first.

Finally, Adam broke the ice.

"You are very beautiful, I have always thought so," he said as he touched his glass against hers in the form of a toast of remembrance for the occasion.

Glory battled to break her glance away from Adam's blue eyes. Everything about him just seemed so perfect to her.

"Why didn't you contact me sooner?" she asked.

Adam puffed out his cheeks.

"Life is never as simple as one makes it out to be," he replied.

"Now that we are finally together, we can make it big as a team, both as a couple and through what we have learnt with our studies."

Glory listened with interest as Adam spoke about several case studies that he had found of huge interest during his archaeology studies. She had always believed that he was no fool and his intellect display had just confirmed that he had a huge future ahead of him – a future that she hoped that she would be a part of.

"If we don't take a chance on us being together, I will consider myself to be a fool," muttered Adam as he changed his glance from Glory's eyes to the table setting of knives and forks in front of him.

Glory wanted to scream the word 'yes', but even if the arena had been empty, she would have still battled to get the word out. For once, Glory Carter was lost for words. The opportunity of being with Adam was right in front of her and her body and voice seemed paralyzed and useless.

Finally, she came to her senses and without thinking, put her left hand on top of his.

"My God, Adam," she said, as she felt a tear of joy begin to trickle down from her right eye.

Adam put his right hand on top of her left.

"It's all good," he remarked.

"Things happen at a certain time in life for a reason. Perhaps the time wasn't right previously but it is now."

Glory looked to the side as if to see which of the students were ready to gossip that she was holding hands with Adam Kennedy. She caught the eye of Deborah Summers, who was now keeping Alan Falcon company much to the annoyance of Jennifer Ellis. Deborah gave her the 'thumbs up' followed by a wink.

The night belonged to Adam and Glory. For them, the time in the Ratner Athletics Center seemed endless as they laughed and danced the night away.

The music played in the centre was divid into decades. The youngsters loved the tracks from singers such as Pitbull, Nicki Minaj, Rhianna, and more, while the teaching staffs of the university seemed to come to life on the dance floor when tracks from the 1980s musicals such as Grease and Saturday Night Fever were played.

Once when seated during a break in dancing, Glory thought about telling Adam about what she had witnessed through the telescope in the laboratory two days before, but the timing just wasn't right. This was Prom Night. She needed to make sure that she would see Adam Kennedy again before all of the final year students went their separate ways. This was not a time to talk about work.

While in the queue to get dinner, Adam left Glory's side momentarily to get another beer, and Jennifer Ellis seized the moment as she charged towards Glory.

"Well aren't we the little slut tonight?" quipped Jennifer.

"I didn't think that Adam was interested in sloppy seconds or thirds or fourths of all the guys that you have been with."

Glory's eyes were raging and Deborah did well to take her friend's drink from her in-case she attempted to toss its contents at Jennifer.

"Just because I dated a lot of guys over the years, doesn't mean that I slept with them," responded Glory.

"There is more to life than just sex, Jennifer, or didn't your parents teach you that?"

Deborah had to hide her smile. She knew how much Glory would have enjoyed making the last remark.

For a moment, it looked like Jennifer was going to lunge forward to punch Glory but she thought better of it. Her university grades weren't great but good enough to pass, and she didn't want to get suspended over a silly girl fight on prom night.

Jennifer turned around and saw Alan Falcon standing behind her.

"Come on, Alan," she quipped, as she attempted to grab the student physicist arm.

"Let's go."

Alan pulled away from her.

"I think you should go, Jennifer," he replied more as a command.

Jennifer's prom night was getting worse by the second. She turned around in a huff and headed off.

By now, Adam had returned from the bar to join Glory in the food queue. Alan stared at him for a few seconds and then walked away without saying a word. He and Adam had never been friends. Perhaps, Adam's bank balance wasn't big enough to get a connection with the Falcon Empire.

"What was the problem?" asked Adam to Glory.

Glory thought for a moment.

"There is no problem, Adam, everything is just fine," she commented.

She introduced Deborah to Adam and he mentioned that he had seen her around at the university campus before.

Deborah giggled.

"That is hard to believe," she said.

"Without these high heel shoes on, my height is pretty much close to that of a midget."

Adam and Glory laughed hysterically. The ice had been broken. Glory had achieved her goal.

With the chance to date Adam, Glory's smile looked even brighter than usual and her green eyes lit up to new proportions. She wasn't a big eater but suddenly realized that she was hungry. The aroma of the spinach soup and roast beef at the buffet was enough to make anyone hungry.

Glory, Adam, and Deborah were now close to the buffet and the black-haired planetology student held her plate of soup close to her chest as if it was a newborn baby.

Once at the buffet stand, she reached forward to put a few ladles of soup into her bowl but it didn't work out that way. Something went wrong. Glory suddenly felt dizzy and her legs began to give way underneath her.

Her plate fell from her hand and hit the Ratner Athletics Center floor before breaking into hundreds of pieces. Soon, Glory's body was on the floor and concerned figures in Adam and Deborah were at her side within seconds.

Adam asked the hordes of bystanders to give them some space while they attended to Glory.

"Glory, what is it?" asked a worried Adam.

Glory tried to lift her head so that she could get to a sitting position but she just didn't have the strength and fell back to a horizontal position on the floor.

"It's that light, it's here in the hall," said a terrified Glory.

"What light, Glory?" inquired Adam.

"It's, it's… it's here, Adam," said Glory, with her hands placed over her face.

"That light is following me."

Adam looked at Deborah who shrugge. Neither were any wiser as to what Glory was talking about.

The university rector, Johnson Matterson called Adam to the side to try to find out what the problem was. Needless to say, Adam could share very little information with the university's No 1.

"Sir, I really don't know what caused Glory to collapse and she is speaking very little sense at the moment," explained Adam to the rector.

"My secretary has called for the paramedics and they should be here any moment," said Johnson Matterson.

While Adam was gone, Glory tried to sit up straight again and succeeded this time.

"The light has gone away, Debbie, it's moved away. I don't know where it came from and how it moved away. I just hope and pray that it never returns. It's scary, Debbie. It's a sign of immense danger to humanity."

Deborah thought that her friend was delusional after the fall and never revealed the latest utterings from Glory to Adam.

Chapter Three

Christmas Eve in Chicago

Monday, 25 December, 10h00

Glory Carter's university days were over and it was time to move into the working woman's role. If she had a job, it would have been a perfect life now that she had found the perfect man.

How would Glory Carter make it as a marketing executive? Her answer was, Terrible.. In fact, anything outside the world of space would not be good for her. Since she was a kid, she had always dreamed of going to space. It was all that really interested her.

With her folder containing her identity and other important documents under her arm, she locked the door to her apartment and headed off to the university's communications office to empty her pigeon post hole for the final time.

On her way back, she noticed a red Aston Marti vehicle driving slowly down the boulevard. She was quick to work out that the driver was staring at her. Most men did that as her beautiful goddess-like looks and model figure was hard to miss.

The Aston Martin vehicle moved closer to her and the driver's window opened.

"Did you need a lift?" said the man behind the wheel.

Glory lifted her sunglasses from her eyes to the top of her head and smiled. The driver was nobody else than Alan Falcon, whom she had never met, but knew by sight.

Glory climbed into the passenger seat next to the driver and ran her hands over the vehicle's plush interior finish. It was like a palace on wheels.

"You must have a sugar mamma who really likes you or else you are doing really well from your tips at your part-time job?" teased Glory.

"Neither," responded Alan.

"I work for my money."

"Work for your money?" replied Glory.

Alan nodded.

"I have been a working man for a few years now."

Glory was stunned. She understood Alan to be a final year student.

"I saw you at the canteen and again at prom night," she said, looking for answers.

Again Alan nodded.

"I was at the university office last week to collect papers," he quipped.

"So what made you go to prom night?" asked Glory.

Alan slowed the Aston Martin down and looked at his passenger.

"I wanted to meet you," he said.

His answer took the wind out of her.

"You know that I am dating Adam Kennedy?" she responded.

Alan continued to drive the vehicle and did not respond to her comment. The last thing he felt like talking about was her fling with Adam Kennedy.

"I work with the US space program."

Glory gasped.

"I thought that the US space program was shut down a few years back?" she queried.

Alan giggled sarcastically.

"Don't believe everything that you read or what the US President tells you."

Glory took her opportunity.

"I have always dreamed of working in a space station ," she said.

"Then give me your Curriculum Vitae and I will see what I can do for you," replied Alan.

Glory remembered that she had her profile in the folder under her arm and took it out before placing it on the dashboard of the Aston Martin near Alan's right arm.

Alan pulled hard on the steering wheel and the vehicle came to a stop near the curbside.

"Isn't this where you live?" he said, in reference to the area which was home to the female students at the University of Chicago.

Glory smiled and exited the vehicle.

"Thanks for the lift, and please don't lose my document," she said.

"If your phone number is on it, I definitely won't lose it," quipped Alan with a smile before winding the window of the driver's door closed and driving off.

Meanwhile, Glory was over the moon with her life. She knew that a big opportunity was just around the corner for her and began to plan her diary with weekly trips to the Observatory Principia which is about four and a half hours drive down the 1-55 S from Chicago.

Even though her university time was over, she spent much time in the library of the tertiary institution as she double-checked her information.

'So the US has a space office that they are not telling the world about?' she thought. The last official US space station, named Skylab, that has no human life onboard, was launched back in 1979.

The Russians were a bit more modern with their space station, Mir, having been active from 1986 to 2001 with three crew members onboard.

Then it was the Chinese, whose 2-person crew onboard, Tiangong 2, was launched on 15 September 2016.

She checked and double checked the information on the internet. There was no sign of any US space station being manufactured or launched over the past few years.

Glory wasn't an expert on the making of space stations but knew that they basically looked like a house. Each space station usually had four to five bedrooms, a kitchen, bathroom, lounge, and sometimes, a gym. There was also a large glass window at the front so that the crew could see space at its best.

Monday, 24 December, 16h00

Glory Carter was hyperactive as she headed towards downtown Chicago to prepare the Christmas Eve meal for the love of her life.

Adam Kennedy was everything that she ever wanted and now there was a chance of Alan Falcon job opportunity for her too. Not too bad for a girl of a middle-class upbringing who hailed originally from Los Angeles.

Once at Adam's flat, she set to work to prepare the special meal. It wasn't long before the smell of pot roast was not only filling Adam's flat but the neighbours too.

Glory was a wiz in the kitchen. She had inherited the cooking skills from her mother, Betsy Carter, but alas, both were found wanting on the baking front. Glory tried her best to make the Apple Crumble pie for pudding, but it became just that – crumble.

At 16h50, Adam Kennedy made his way through the front door. He knew that his timing had to be spot on as he had some bad news for Glory.

He knew how excited she was about the two of them spending their first Christmas together. Now due to work commitments, he had to burst her bubble.

Adam sniffed in the awesome aroma of pot roast as he entered his apartment. Yeah, it was great to have a woman in his life and even more so, the right one.

"Honey, don't outdo yourself," he said to Glory as he gave her a hug and passionate kiss.

"I can't believe that this is our first Christmas together," she said with excitement.

Adam smiled but opted to eat supper first before breaking the bad news.

Once seated in the lounge with a quality plate of food in front of him, Adam felt like a king.

The apple crumble pudding was divine and not nearly as bad as it looked.

"So what are we doing on Christmas Day?" asked Glory.

Adam nearly choked on his last mouthful of apple crumble at the question.

He cleared his throat not that it would make the impact of his news any less devastating.

"Honey... I have to go on a mission tomorrow. I can't say too much about it as its government clearance stuff."

Glory looked up from her tray of food.

"You are joking, right? Adam, tell me that you are joking."

Adam sighed.

"Honey, you know how my work schedule goes," remarked Adam.

Glory was distraught.

"You promised we would be together for Christmas?"

Adam shrugged his shoulders.

"Everything was just fine until I got a call this afternoon," he explained.

"Think about it this way; its money in the bank for us."

Glory wiped the tears of frustration from her eyes. It was a battle that she clearly wasn't going to win. Then she said something that she wished she hadn't.

"Is your work part of the US space mission?"

Adam looked up at his girlfriend.

"Honey, you know that the US space station project closed down a few years back. It's another project that I am busy with."

Adam knew that he couldn't divulge his mission, not even to Glory. If it ever came out that he had breached security information protocol, it basically equalled treason.

Glory packed the supper plates and pudding bowls into the dishwasher. Something deep down inside told her that Adam might be away for quite some days. She hoped that her gut feeling was wrong.

She led Adam towards the Christmas tree which was in the corner of the lounge opposite the fireplace and picked up a small, well-wrapped package, which she handed to him.

Adam was not usually an emotional man but he had to hold himself together when he unwrapped the packaging of the gift and saw a top-of-the-range Audemars Piguet wristwatch in front of him.

"Honey, this must have cost a fortune and I don't want you to spend all your cash on me," he said.

Glory grinned.

"I wanted to show you how special you are to me, Adam. Make sure you wear it whenever you go on your mission."

Adam pointed to a huge wrapped up box next to the Christmas tree.

After receiving the Audemars Piguet from Glory, he suddenly felt cheap over his gift to her. He had worked really hard since Prom Night to find the right gift for her

Glory began to unwrap her big box and her eyes lit up when she saw the contents.

"Encyclopedias on the solar system!" she screamed.

"I love it, Adam. It's better than any other gift I could have wished for."

Adam giggled.

"I didn't want to get you a food mixer," he teased.

"You get me a food mixer or a blender and we are through mister," joked Glory.

"Encyclopedias are better value for information than any internet site will ever be."

Phew, thought Adam as he wiped his brow. Perhaps he wasn't so cheap after all.

Glory took Adam by the hand and led him to the bedroom. Tonight was the night that she would offer up her virginity to Mr Right.

Adam didn't resist too much! Soon, he was naked on his back with her on top of him in a seated position. She undid her blouse and removed it. Glory remembered her no sex before marriage policy, but sometimes policies need to be overlooked.

Gloria dreamed of this all her life. She wanted it so badly. It was an honest and sincere desire. This landscape and this picture often came to her in a dream. She constantly thought about it. She could not believe it until now. This is no longer a dream. This is her life. It's true.

The soul sings. All parts of her body love Adam. She is in heaven with happiness.

She didn't resist when Adam gently pulled her onto his thighs. She tilted her head backwards as he leaned down to kiss her neck. He trailed sweet kisses from her neck down to the swell of her luscious, young breasts. She cried out his name, threading her fingers through his hair as he cupped her breasts.

He looked into her eyes, gently asking for permission and she nodded her head. He trailed feather-light kisses over her neck, shoulders, and arms. He pampered every part of her body, a nibble here, and a love bite there. He kissed her lips, tracing every contour of her lips with his tongue while whispering softly into her ears. He made sweet love to her in the open, declaring his undying love for her.

His hands unclasped her bra, and his tongue circled her bared nipple, he bit, suckled and licked them until she couldn't take it anymore. His hand had stolen into her skirt at one point, and it found its way into her warm and moist slit. He slipped a finger into her and slowly moved within her with his fingers. He was so gentle with her that she wanted to cry out. He brought her to orgasm twice with only his fingers. When she gave him her permission to explore her body further, he slipped off his pant and widened her legs. He gave her three more orgasms before he shot his semen deep into her. She would never forget those hot nights in his arms. Adam murmured in her ear, kissing her lips softly. He kissed her tenderly and with passion. He gently nibbled on her tender earlobes, eliciting a moan from her. Her heart was beating wildly in her chest as he nibbled softly at her ear with tongue, slipping his tongue into the crevice of her ear. Glory slowly opened her eyes, tilting her face up as his mouth closed over hers. She trembled as his warm tongue found hers. He trailed a finger, tantalizingly along her jawline and downwards to the swell of her breasts. He deepened the kiss as she moaned into his mouth. He tore his mouth away from hers, staring into her misty eyes.

"Glory, you are so beautiful," Adam gasped.

She was too choked up with emotions to reply. Adam always made her feel beautiful and desirable. Her heart swelled with love for him, and the tears in her eyes were tears of happiness. She was the luckiest and happiest woman on earth. She arched her back in ecstasy as Adam gently cupped her aching breasts. Her moan grew louder as he gently grazed the pad of his thumb over her nipples.

"You are so beautiful," he murmured huskily again and slipped his tongue into her mouth.

They kissed passionately while their hands explored each other's body. His hard mouth grounded against hers in a hot searing kiss. She made a throaty sound, gently widening her legs for him. He placed sweet kisses on the swell of her breasts to the flat plane of her stomach. His fingers found and played with the curly dark hairs at the juncture of her thighs.

She cried out when his fingers found her throbbing, sensitive spot. He slipped his fingers into her, kissing her lips, face, and eyes. She was so beautiful and angelic that he wanted to please every part of her. He gently parted her legs...

It felt like Adam had literally just closed his eyes when the alarm on his mobile phone went off. It was 04h15 and he needed to rise and get ready to head off to work.

He looked at Glory. She looked even more beautiful when she was sleeping.

He took a shower, shaved, and dressed up for work. Before grabbing his backpack and briefcase, he pulled the duvet cover over Glory and kissed her gently on the forehead in order not to wake her.

Adam Kennedy was a man on a mission. He never knew when he would be coming back. He never knew if he would be coming back.

If only he could take Glory with him. No. That's a bad idea, he thought. Then she wouldn't know when she would be returning either.

Glory rolled over on the bed and looked for a moment as if she was going to wake up.

Adam knew that he had to leave – it was now or never!

He took one last look at her. God, he hoped he was doing the right thing!

Chapter Four

Barefoot and Pregnant

Glory Carter dressed in a dressing gown and barefoot, stared into the mirror above a small desk in the bedroom of Adam Kennedy's apartment. Her emotions were running wild.

Yeah, she had received a video message from Adam who stated that he was well and working hard at the mission, but he wasn't able to provide her with a date of his possible return.

Glory had another potential problem on her hands too. She had missed her period and was providing stalling tactics. 'Oh, my God, I can't be pregnant, surely,' she thought.

She needed to speak to someone who would be able to keep her secret. Glory picked up her mobile.

"Debbie, how has the new year treated you so far?"

Deborah Summers, back at her parents' home in Dallas, Texas, was pleased to hear from her friend.

"Is Adam back yet?" asked Deborah.

"No, and I just have this feeling that it could be another few weeks or months before he returns," answered Glory.

"As long as he stays in contact with me and I know that he is alright, I will have peace of mind. Besides, as Adam always says, the more he works; the more money in the bank."

"Do you know where he is?" pressed Deborah.

Glory was becoming even more and more certain that her boyfriend was on a space mission, but she couldn't get confirmation on that, when the US Presidency had made it clear that the country had closed down its space operations a few years back.

"I haven't got a clue where Adam is, but he contacted me to say that all is well with him," replied Glory.

"However, this is not the reason that I am calling you. Debbie, I skipped my period a few days back."

Deborah gasped.

"Glory, do you think that you are 'PG'?"

"Possibly, Debbie, I am vomiting a bit and eating like a horse. Also, I am feeling tired in the afternoons which is unlike me."

Debbie was so excited as if it was her that was pregnant.

"Glory, I am telling you that you are 'PG'. All the symptoms are there. I mean, I am presuming that you made love to Adam before he left?"

"Yeah, on Christmas Eve," responded Glory.

"So why don't you do the at-home pregnancy test to find out for sure?" questioned the girl from Texas.

Glory Carter remained silent for a moment.

"Deborah, I am afraid," she quipped.

"I mean, I don't even know if Adam wants kids. We never had a chance to discuss those finer details of life."

Deborah made a clicking noise with her tongue as she thought.

"Well, either way, you need to find out," she said.

"It's one of two ways. Either you do the home pregnancy test or go straight to the hospital. They will tell you for sure."

Glory agreed.

"Let me go to the hospital and find out," she said.

"I don't trust these home pregnancy tests which have a chance of error when one has raised expectations. I promise you will be the first to know either way."

Glory took a shower and let the warm water run over her beautiful face and body, as she went into a deep-in-thought trance.

Was her life a dream? Did she really finish her planetology degree at the University of Chicago? Did she really meet Adam Kennedy? Did she get offered a potential job opportunity by Alan Falcon? Was she about to become a mother?

She dressed and made her way across the city to the North western Memorial Hospital at 251 E Huron Street.

As she walked in through the main entrance of the hospital, she saw a long queue of pregnant women waiting for their turn to see the on-duty gynaecologists.

Glory had never been to a gynaecologist in her life as she had never been sexually active before. She had heard horror stories from some of her more promiscuous girlfriends, who explained in utmost detail of how they hated going for such check-ups and what the doctors did to them according to medical practice.

How she wished that she had a background in karate. If the doctor, male or female, put a hand too deep into a sensitive area of her body, she would have sorted the problem out with a kung-fu move.

Her mind returned to reality and after a two-hour wait in the queue, she got her chance to be examined. A female gynaecologist, Dr

Blanche Miller examined her. Thank God, she thought, a female doctor!

Forty minutes later, Glory Carter walked out of the doctor's consulting room filled with more mixed emotions. Pregnant she was, with a huge possibility of being the mother to twins in just over eight months from now.

She had promised to tell Deborah Summers first but she knew that she needed to tell Adam. The problem was that there was just no way for her to get hold of him. When he sent video messages to her, it was a one-way communication. He could contact her, but she had no way to contact him.

As for her parents, they were very old-fashioned. Pre-marital sex was out of the question as far as they were concerned. So too was living with a boyfriend, which is why Glory had to tell her mother that she was rooming with one of her former student girlfriends, not with the love of her life.

Saturday arrived and the sound of an incoming message on her mobile phone awoke Glory Carter as she lay on the double bed in Adam Kennedy's flat.

Yeah! It's a video message from Adam. The speed of work on the mission had increased and he felt that he would be home sooner than expected. Unfortunately, he still could not provide a date or time for his return from the secret mission.

Glory played the video recording over and over again. She could see that her man was in good health and that he spoke with a great sense of confidence. His mood seemed to be upbeat

Her heart pained just to have five words for him. Those would have been 'Pregnant with twins. Love you'.

Life had never been easy for Glory Carter. It seemed like one challenge followed by the next. Sometimes, she felt like the more she prayed, the worse things got. Most of her girlfriends had given up on church. Now in their early twenties, partying until the early hours of Sunday morning was the thing to do and then to get up four or five hours later to go to worship was just too big an ask.

Glory Carter's life changed forever in the space of a few minutes as she gave birth to her twins, Adam Jnr and Rachel, at the Northwestern Memorial Hospital.

At her bedside was her mother Betsy and her father Conroy, who had not spoken a word to his daughter since he found out that she was pregnant out of wedlock. Conroy, now in his late fifties, was a prominent insurance broker and a church deacon. He felt that he needed to keep his daughter's out-of-wedlock birth silent to avoid embarrassment to his image.

Betsy meanwhile, was just too happy to become a grandmother, and was open to telling anyone who was keen to hear.

Also at Glory's bedside was Deborah Summers who had made the trip from Texas to share in this life-changing moment with her friend.

What Glory could never share with her parents was the amount of crying that she had done over the past few months due to the absence of Adam. Communication from Adam Kennedy had now become far too irregular. Instead of once-a-week video messages, Glory received his communication once every two months or more.

Prior to the childbirth, Deborah had put Glory's wrinkled skin, in particular under her eyes, down to motherhood stress, but soon found out from her friend that it was all down to the worry over the father of her children.

Adam never even knew that he was going to be a father or even that he had become one. Although, it was not the faulof Glory.

Time was ticking and Glory's life was changing rapidly by the minute. Since Adam's departure, she had managed to get a job as a salesperson at a leading boutique chain-store not far from where she stayed. The pay was good too and her mother had been of great help by spending much time in Chicago at the apartment. Needless to say, her father hadn't put a foot in the city, and Glory had made Betsy Carter promise not to reveal a word about her staying place to him.

Glory Carter is leading a hectic life. At least, the kids are keeping her mind of Adam's absence, but the absence is now too long. She hasn't heard from him for a few months and had even approached the local police station. The officers on duty were keen to open a 'Missing Persons' case until Glory told them that Adam was on a US governmental mission.

This seemed to scare the boys in blue off and they refused to help her. Neither of the cops on duty was ranked high enough or had enough experience to know how to report a case to the American FBI investigators.

Glory was just taking a chance by approaching the police. How could she be sure that Adam was indeed missing?

"Glory!" screamed Betsy Carter from the lounge.

"Check your Tablet computer! I think its Adam!"

Glory left the twins in their crib and charged into the lounge of Adam's apartment.

She pushed the 'Enter' button on her Tablet and waited. It seemed like an eternity before the video message started to play.

Adam suddenly appeared on the screen of her device. He looked thin and weak. His speech was also disjointed. Again, Adam mentioned that he wasn't sure when he would be returning home Something was seriously wrong on the mission!

If it was any form of comfort to Glory, at least she knew that Adam was still alive and trying to make contact with her.

His last words on the message sent a chill down her spine.

"Whatever you do, Glory, don't contact the government or the law enforcement agencies. This is a top-secret mission".

Glory burst into tears and her mother moved over to console her daughter.

"Something is wrong, Ma," said the new mother of twins.

"Look at Adam!"

Besty Carter did her best to lift the spirits of her daughter and offered to take Glory and the twins out for coffee and chocolate cake.

Glory had just finished feeding and changing the diapers of the twins on Thursday afternoon when Betsy yelled that another incoming video message from Adam was awaiting downloading on her daughter's Tablet computer.

With a baby on each arm, Glory rushed to the lounge and again pushed 'Enter' on her Tablet. If only Adam could see their children. Adam Jnr looked like a younger version of him while Rachel would almost certainly turn out to be a carbon copy of her mother.

This time, there was no video footage but an audio message only.

'We regret to inform family and friends of the secret mission that all involved with the project have been lost. While the loss of human life has not yet been confirmed, we request your patience over the next few days as our agencies attempt to trace the whereabouts of your loved ones. We thank you in advance for your patience in this regard. 1416'.

Glory did not even have enough energy left in her body to cry. She began to shout out the keywords of the message.

"'Lost! Trace! Patience!'"

Again, Betsy Carter attempted to console her daughter and took the twins from her when it looked like Glory was about to collapse with them to the floor.

"Adam!" screamed Glory at her Tablet computer in the hope that her boyfriend could hear her.

"I need you! Your kids need you!"

She turned to Betsy.

"He is alive, Ma. I know he is. He is out there!"

Chapter Five

Adam's Disappearing Act sinks in

Monday, 29 October, 18h00

Glory was in a state of shock. She played the latest message over and over again and each time, it felt like she was on the brink of having a heart attack. Betsy had made her daughter's favourite meal for supper – lasagna.

"You should have been born Italian," the mother often said to her daughter over the years, as a young Glory gulped down the pasta food. This time though, Glory hardly touched her dinner and Betsy could fully understand.

The mother picked up the remote control for the television set.

"Should I change the channel to 14 for the news?" she asked.

Suddenly, something as powerful as the light ray that she had seen back in the university laboratory, hit Glory. She felt like she had been hit by a baseball bat as an idea went through her head.

Of course, Glory, she thought and switched on her Tablet computer to replay the message that she had received.

"Oh, darling, you are not going to listen to the message again, are you?" asked Betsy, as she tried to get her daughter's attention away from the unfolding drama for a few hours.

"Ma, you said '14' for the channel," remarked Glory.

"Well, what are these 1416 digits at the end of the message?"

Betsy shrugged her shoulders.

"I don't know, you are the one with the brains in this family."

Glory shook her head.

"No, it must mean something. It is a sign," she said.

Betsy did not want to get her daughter's hopes up.

"It could be just some sort of computer coding to get the message to you," said the mother.

Again Glory shook her head aggressively.

"No, Ma, it's some sort of secret message from Adam. I know it is!"

The conversation was interrupted by the ringing of the doorbell.

Betsy Carter went to the door and welcomed the visitor. Glory's heart skipped a beat.

"Was it Adam?"

"Oh, hello, Alan Falcon," she said with a slight smile, as the physicist appeared in the doorway.

Dressed in a light blue suit, Alan was on a mission. The bunch of red roses in his right hand was proof of this.

"I will give you two some space," said Betsy, as she collected the twins and took them to the bedroom.

Once the older woman had left the lounge, Alan held the bunch of roses out towards Glory.

"These flowers will never be as beautiful as you are," began Alan.

Glory tried to cut him short.

"Alan, stop, you know I am in a relationship with…"

"Adam is gone, Glory," he said.

"He is never coming back. So what do you want to do? Sit around and dream for the rest of your days of what could have been. I have loved you since the first time that I laid my eyes on you. It is fate that is drawing us together. Don't you understand that?"

Glory's top lip began to get the jitters.

"Alan, I have twins with Adam and he will come back one day. I know he will." she said.

Alan sat down on the sofa next to Glory as she stared at him more with different emotions going through her mind.

"Glory, if only you know about my life history," he said in a serious tone.

"I was never one of the popular boys at school and used to be bullied," he began.

"Then when my parents divorced, I was physically and emotionally abused by my mother's new boyfriend when we moved in with him. Life was hell, Glory. However, I believe that my luck is now changing."

He put a hand on each of Glory's shoulders.

"Marry me, Glory and I will give you whatever your heart desires," pleaded Alan.

"Money is not a problem. As for your kids, I am impotent and can't have children so your young ones will be mine too. Just say yes, Glory, please, just say yes. I don't want to live my life alone. I need a family around me."

Glory's heart was pumping with emotions.

"What about Adam?" she asked in a squeaky voice.

"Glory, Adam is gone," summarized Alan.

"If he was alive, then he would have made contact with you by now. Think about it, Glory. You and I can be so good together. There is no challenge that will be too great for us to surpass."

Glory stood up from the sofa.

She was caught in two minds. Her love for Adam was one thing but everything else that Alan was saying made complete sense. She couldn't wait and waste her life away. What if, as Alan eluded too, Adam never came back?

"Alan, please give me a day or two to think about it, ok?" she asked.

Alan nodded.

"I know it's a big decision and I won't rush you," he said as he stood up and embraced her before kissing her gently on the cheek.

"I will wait to hear from you," he concluded and left the room.

"Don't worry, I will see myself out."

Glory heard the front door of the apartment shut behind Alan and his footsteps on the tiled corridor floor as he headed away.

Alan Falcon was so gentle and kind, Glory thought.

If Adam was indeed missing forever, Alan would be the perfect next in line for her. But was the father of the twins really gone?

Glory sighed. She never discussed the contents of her meeting with her mother. Betsy Carter wasn't a nosy person and didn't even probe her daughter on the chat in the lounge.

For the next two days, Glory Carter thought the Adam/Glory and Alan/Glory scenario through from every possible angle.

Eventually, she had to concede that Alan was right. If Adam was alive, he would have made contact with her by now. After all, he had been gone for a few months now.

She picked up her mobile phone and dialled Alan's number.

"Alan Falcon, its Mrs Falcon-to-be here, when is our wedding date?"

Alan shrieked with excitement while holding his mobile phone on the other end of the call.

"I am glad you came to your senses, Glory," he said.

"It is for the best, believe me. We will be magical together."

Four weeks later, Glory Carter became Mrs Glory Falcon in front of 1000 family and friends at the Holy Name Cathedral in Wabash Avenue, which was followed by a glitz and glamour reception. Glory and Alan danced the night away until their feet ached. Love was indeed in the air. Both were moving forward with their lives!

Betsy and Conroy Carter watched on. The mother had tears of joy in her eyes as she believed that after all that she had heard and all that her daughter had been through, she had finally found the right man to build her life with.

Conroy's greying moustache left one to wonder if he was smiling or not. He had never met Adam Kennedy and had engaged with Alan Falcon for a small amount of time.

If anything made him happy, it was the fact that his daughter now had a wedding ring on her finger. Those who didn't know the whole story would at least think that the husband was the father of her twins.

Fortunately, Glory couldn't hear what some guests were saying about her, be it out of pure gossip or jealousy.

"Well, Glory won't have to work another day of her life," said one elderly woman to a plump middle-aged lady sitting next to her.

"Yeah, she fell with her proverbial backside in the butter, didn't she? She is a real Cinderella. From rags to bloody riches, I'll say."

Of course, none of the woman or any other guests in the room knew exactly what Alan did for a living, but having seen his Aston Martin car and suits, it was quite clear that he was pretty high up in management in some company or organization.

Little did these old women know that Glory Falcon had every intention of working. There was enough money to get a housekeeper to look after the twins during the day, while the mother of the kids followed her dream of being involved in a space program. Surely, her husband could pull a few strings. After all, she had given him her CV some months back when he had given her a lift home in his Aston Martin car.

Now there was even more reason for Alan to fast-track a position for her on the program which was based at Cape Canaveral, Florida, near the centre of the state's Atlantic coast.

The bride and groom made their way around the room as they greeted all the guests. Glory's bridesmaid was none other than Deborah Summers, dressed in a slick white ball gown.

Glory turned to Deborah and grinned.

"Did you ever foresee this happening, Debbie? she said.

"It is amazing how life often takes one in different directions."

Except for two cousins, and Alan's mother, Thelma, very few of Alan's family had even responded to his wedding invitation. The Falcon family was not as closely knit as the Kennedys.

As far as the Kennedy family was concerned, every man and his dog were present. Even those who weren't that close to Glory had made the trip for a free night's accommodation and meal at Alan's expense. You guessed it, the freeloaders were members of Conroy Kennedy's side of the family.

Glory's distant cousin Clifford, had just made it through high school and worked as a messenger at a local community newspaper in Chicago. For him, this was a step up. He would never own an Aston Martin in this lifetime, but his luck may change if he rubbed shoulders with the rich and famous at Alan Falcon's wedding.

Betsy's sister, Getrude, was no angel either. She had always wanted her two children to succeed in life and wished only the worst for her sister's kids. Now Glory was the star that was shining brightly while Gertrude's daughter Denise and son, Frank, had been through nasty divorces.

Sometimes, what you wish upon other people comes right back to haunt your own life.

Nobody in the room, besides Glory and to a lesser extent, Alan and Deborah, had ever met Adam Kennedy, so few even broached the subject.

Glory had done well to make sure her University of Chicago nemesis, Jennifer Ellis, wasn't invited. Otherwise, Adam Kennedy would have been the talk of the wedding for sure.

Deborah Summer stared at her friend who was greeting people in the distance. Glory's face was absolutely glowing. Deborah had never seen her friend this happy before and her gut feeling told her that Alan Falcon was the perfect match for the bride.

Perhaps, it was the work of the man upstairs in the heavens who had decided that Adam Kennedy was the wrong one for Glory. Deborah was a firm believer that things happen for a reason in life.

It was almost time for Glory to throw her garter. As is the custom at weddings, the unmarried ladies would line up and the bride would stand with her back towards them before throwing her garter over her head. The lady who catches the garter is deemed the next one likely to get married.

Whistles went up from the men around the room as Alan disappeared under Glory's dress in an attempt to get the garter off her and then gave it to his bride.

Glory Falcon tossed the elastic garter over her head and as luck would have it, Deborah Summers made the catch amid a scramble from over thirty females.

Deborah blushed as Glory grinned at her.

Deborah still had no love interest on the horizon but remembered her friend's words.

"It is amazing how life often takes one in different directions."

Glory erupted into a loud laugh. Alan loved that laughter. He was crazy about it. He loved her strongly, and he could never get enough of loving her. She was his heartbeat and the light to his soul. She was the first and only girl to stir something in his heart. Glory tugged at his heartstrings, making him want all the things he never thought he would have. A home, Happiness, and Heaven on earth. She thought she wasn't beautiful because her thighs were plump and her lips were full. She sometimes complained about her looks but when he looked at her, he only saw a sexy girl with pretty eyes. He loved every bit of her and he wished he could rip his heart out so she could see how strongly it beat for her.

Her laughter made him want to laugh. Her sweet voice was melody to his ears. Beautiful, sexy, and smart Glory with a terrific sense of humour. Alan always wondered how he ever got so lucky, she could light up his world with just a smile. She knew him better than he knew himself and she was always there for him. Her presence was like a soothing balm to his soul. If he could, he would place the moon at her feet but his Glory wouldn't want that. She wouldn't want all the riches and glories of the world either. No, no, she wasn't that type of girl. She would ask for their simple life which was filled with happiness. Walking through each day and scooping her into his arms will gladden her heart. Her eyes glowed radiantly each time one of the twins called him 'daddy'. He could give her diamonds, pearls, and rubies but his love, kisses, and touch were the things she craved for. But Alan could not give Glory children. Alan was sterile. He thought that God had arranged all this for him. Fate gave him Glory with the children. Alan was grateful to God for that.

Glory leaned over and kissed Alan's lips, breaking into his reverie.

"Glory!" He said, as she lightly pinched his nipples.

"I love you," She murmured naughtily, as she tentatively licked his jaw, placing soft kisses all over his handsome face.

He thought she had the prettiest eyes in the world. He could never get tired of gazing at them. Alan kissed Glory. Glory was in the power of Alan already. She buried her nose in the crook of his neck, inhaling the clean scent of his aftershave, a masculine scent of soap and shampoo. The warmth emanating from his body soothed her and she snuggled closer to him. Her heart squeezed painfully with love for him. He sets her on fire with just a look and right now she was burning for him. Every part of her cried out for his love and touch. She held his handsome face in her palms, gently planting her soft lips on his. A tremor ran through her as he took control of the kiss. She moaned into his mouth, arching her back as a ripple of pleasure went through her. Her legs were quivering as passion stole into their kiss. Her love for him waxed stronger and stronger with each passing day until she felt that she couldn't go a day without his sweet kisses.

His hot tongue explored the roof of her mouth, eliciting moans from her. She was in heaven. The tip of his tongue continued to search the delicate insides of her lips while his hands gently caressed her body.

He wove his hands through her glossy hair, lightly caressing it. Alan trailed kisses from her neck to her boobs. Her breasts were only a handful but they were round, soft, and pretty. They were a bit saggy and there were streaks of pale stretch marks on them but he told her that they were beautiful. Those breasts had nursed babies and he thought she was so strong to nurse two babies at the same time. Her nipples were long, pink, and puffy with dark areolas. He gently teased her nipples with his fingers until they grew harder.

"I love you Glory," said Alan.

"I love you, Alan," She moaned.

He gently worried her nipple between his teeth, grazing on the tips with his tongue. He sucked on each hard peak for a minute before trailing a tingly path from her belly button down to the curly hairs between her thighs. He combed his fingers through her silky pubic hair as his mouth sought out hers again. He massaged her mound, making her moan with pleasure. He kissed every part of her body, murmuring endearments to her. Glory caressed his muscled chest and backs. Tears stung her eyes as she realized that her home was wherever this man was. The home was where her heart belonged and her home was with Alan.

"My love, are you okay?" Alan asked in a husky voice. He had noticed the change in her, she was clinging to his body like they were saying goodbyes. "We will never be apart again my love, we will always be together from now on," Sometimes he was scared that he might lose her. He wondered just how far he would go to keep her in his life, he will do anything to keep her in his life, even if it means losing his own life in the process.

"Is that a promise?" She asked in a choked voice.

"I promise," Alan said

He kissed every part of her body, murmuring endearments to her. He kissed his way down from her creamy white belly down to her thighs. He leaned his head forward and kissed Glory's breasts, softly, pressing kisses all over it. She moaned as Alan slowly kissed his way around her breasts, twirling his tongue on the tip of her tender nipples. When he finally entered her warm sheath, he felt like he had died and gone to heaven. The pleasure was too much for Glory that she could only moan. Waves of orgasm washed over her and he continued to pleasure her until she thought that she would die of pleasure...

Alan is forgiving her because she called out Adam's name when they were making love. Afterwards, they slept in each other's arms, listening to   the   sound   of   each   other's   heartbeat.

Chapter Six

In Florida, in Love

Six months later, Glory Falcon's body and life had changed dramatically.

Not that she was pregnant again, but her usually tender legs were developing muscles from all the climbing of the stairs in the family's plush double story home in Cocoa Beach on the island just off the Florida coast.

The twins, as small as they were, were living their new lives. Adam Jnr was eating like a horse and looked much bigger and older than he was six months ago. While young Rachel was a splitting image of her mother.

Glory was as happy as could be but not a day or hour went by when she did not wonder what had happened to Adam Kennedy.

Alan Falcon was so good to his wife and showered her and the kids with gifts not only on their birthdays but on other occasions too.

When they moved into the new house, Alan and Glory had made a pact not to mention the word 'Adam'. It was time to move forward with their lives and the twins hadn't even met their biological father.

She had always sensed that her husband might know more about Adam's disappearance than he let on, but she kept her side of the bargain.

Like Adam had been about information regarding his secret mission, Alan was just as tight-lipped about what was going on with his project at the space station at Cape Canaveral which was a few miles away from our home on the island.

On the odd occasion when she had dared to enter into the foreign territory to speak about her husband's work, Alan had clammed up pretty quickly. What could be so secretive that would make a family man not reveal a word about what he does between 9 am and 5 pm to his wife and kids?

One day when Alan was at work, Glory left the twins in the safe hands of her domestic housekeeper, Joey Lawrence, and went upstairs to the study room.

From her days as a student, she had always wanted to make a trip to the Paranal Observatory, which was situated in the Atacama Desert of northern Chile on Cerro Paranal mountain range at about 8645 feet above sea level.

The observatory's head Professor, Alejandro Goic, had been instrumental in the development of the 26.9 feet reflector, known internationally as the Very Large Telescope.

Over the past few months, Glory had not experienced that sharp light that had struck her in the University of Chicago's laboratory and the Ratner Athletics Center on Prom Night.

Glory was adamant that there was something beyond Planet Earth, perhaps even life forms. She was even more convinced that Alan probably knew more about this than he was letting on. If her husband worked with space programs on a daily basis, surely he had been privileged to see some strange or not so strange things?

Glory got hold of the telephone number for the Paranal Observatory and placed a call from her mobile phone. She was fully aware that language was about to become an issue as most Chilean spoke more Spanish than English. Glory had achieved straight 'A's' for Spanish in her high school years but that seemed like a lifetime ago now. Besides, there is a big difference between writing a Spanish exam and actually speaking the language.

'Hola,' said the person on the other end of the line.

Glory did her best in what was her third language after English and French, another language that she studied in high school.

Eventually, she got put through to another department at the observatory where a lady answered. Fortunately for Glory, the person on the other end of the call could speak fairly fluent English.

"Ms Glory, you want to speak to the Professor?" she said in a timid voice.

"Haven't you heard the news? Professor Goic died in a car accident on the Paranal mountain range three months ago. It was so sad. He worked here for thirty-seven years."

Glory gasped. Was she now out of teaching with the goings-on in planetology and observatories that she didn't even know that one of the greatest Professors on the space scene of all time had passed on?

"I am so sorry to hear that," she said.

"By all accounts, the Professor was a wonderful man and an extremely clever person."

"Clever?" exclaimed the lady.

"Did you say clever? He was nothing short of a genius. It will be another one hundred or two hundred years before this observatory has someone of his ability and commitment again."

"How did he pass away?" questioned Glory.

"Was it sudden?"

The lady began to sob.

"His car went over the edge of the mountain cliff," she said.

"It is very strange as the Professor was a careful driver. He always drove slowly and everyone at the observatory teased him about that. I think there may have been… wait let me stop before I say too much."

Glory could feel her face going cold and a chilly sweat began to drip from her forehead.

"Ma'am, you don't think that someone…"

"Look, I have worked here at the observatory for over seven years as the assistant to the Professor and I know that he was threatened on a few occasions on some of his views and findings. I hope you weren't contacting him about possibly getting into the space program, were you?"

"Well actually…" said Glory before she was cut short.

"Don't if you know what is good for you," the lady went on.

"I was like you when I was young. I dreamed of going to space and when I finally got the chance to work in the observatory, I saw a whole different, evil side of this industry. The end of the world is not as far away as you think. You see, now you make me speak too much. I need to go."

"Wait, why do you say that the end of the world is not far off?" asked Glory.

"Ask your fellow Americans at Cape Canaveral," said the lady.

"I speak too much. I must go. Adios."

The phone went dead in Glory's ear and she put it down next to her.

She wasn't sure what the woman was eluding, but her evasiveness to keep her lips tied with the cold shoulder style was like the deep secrecy shown by Alan Falcon about his secret mission at the space office at Cape Canaveral. There must be a link between the two.

Glory wasn't even worried about her own life. She had two infants to worry about. Within an hour, Glory Falcon, neatly dressed in a blue blouse and black slacks, was seated inside a cab on her way to Alan Falcon's office at Cape Canaveral.

Once at the space campus, Glory's mind was blown away. It took no less than ten security checks before she got anywhere near Alan's office. What was so secretive that the mission had to have more security procedures in place than those guarding the US President?

A young administration clerk eventually escorted her to Alan Falcon's office.

Alan sat at his desk and looked up from the document that he was reading. He smiled instantly and then refrained himself as he made his way over to his wife. He was caught between a 'honey, I am so pleased to see you' to a 'what are you doing here? What will my work colleagues think when they see my wife here?'

He shut the door and embraced Glory before giving her a passionate kiss.

With the niceties done with, Glory fired the opening question.

"Honey, what is up with Armageddon?"

Alan wiped his brow with his handkerchief.

"What do you mean?" he inquired.

Glory explained about her telephone call to the observatory in Chile and what the woman had told her.

Alan sighed and stared at his wife, before ushering her to a seat in front of his desk.

"Honey, I will try and explain it all to you but please don't interrupt me as the information is quite sensitive and can be complicated at times."

"According to legend, which Adam also knew, people were made as helpers to the gods, basically a workforce. People on earth have destroyed how things should have been. Think about it: war, nuclear tests, biological weapons, carbon dioxide…"

Alan went on.

"Armageddon as you call it is coming soon. We refer to it as 'Planet X and it is heading straight for Planet Earth. It will melt all glaciers and unleash hunger, epidemics, and radiation. The radiation stream will destroy all forms of life on earth."

Glory stared at her husband who looked mentally drained from all the hours that he had put into his work over the past few months.

"When the radiation strikes on X-Ray Day, it is all over here on earth. So we have been building space crafts to transport human beings to other planets for their own safety."

Alan took in a sip of coffee from a mug that was positioned on his desk and then continued.

Children and parents fall under my protection," he explained and then went around to hug his wife.

"Honey, I don't want to live alone. I don't want to die alone. We need to move as soon as possible before it is too late. As earthlings, we are late to discover the real value of living on other planets. Let's say that we are poor at real estate market evaluation in other parts of the solar system."

"I know that you will have dozens of questions to ask, but please understand that I have been sharing information with you that is not for the eyes and ears of the average man in the street," continued Alan.

"The US military and their Russian counterparts have spent billions of cash working on this project. It is for the good of every human being here on earth but it could only be activated when everything is 100 percent cast in stone. Time is against us, yes, but we will have enough time to activate the plan before Planet-X strikes. Think of it as a UFO heading straight for earth. A collision is imminent."

Tears began to flow down Glory's cheeks.

"It's not as bad as it may seem at first, honey," said Alan.

"Who knows, maybe our twins will be happier living on Mars than here on earth. We can't make that judgment on their behalf. You need to go and I need to get back to my work."

Glory stood up from her seat and smiled at Alan. She knew him to be a workaholic – a man who would do whatever was best for his family and country.

She left the office with many unanswered questions going through her mind. How did this fit in with Adam's mission and did someone at the Paranal Observatory want to stop the process and the first point of call was to shut the Professor up for good? Had he stumbled on some information that could tarnish the space program's plan either way or was she being cynical? Perhaps the Professor had died of natural cause after all. Glory shook her head. The death of the driver of a car that went over the mountain cliff could hardly be put down to 'natural causes'.

Her mind drifted back to her twins. She didn't care about her life or even that of Alan at the moment. Her children came first and if there were only two seats left on one of the spaceships to Mars, then she would definitely offer the places to Adam Jnr and Rachel. They were the future, while she and Alan was the present.

It almost seemed like the security checks that had to be undertaken to leave the building, were nearly as much as when she came in. Were the US and Russian military worried that she might leave with a spaceship in her pocket? The security elements looked silly to her.

Chapter Seven

Life is a Beach

The sun was setting as Glory Falcon sat deep in her thought, looking out over the Coca Beach coastline. The yellow cab was close to reaching its destination and aaccomplishing the request of returning her home.

Life can be a beach, thought Glory. Yeah, life can also be a bitch.

Heaven, the smash pop hit of Bryan Adams from the 1980s, was playing over the car radio. Glory shook her head. Heaven... Good, honest Professor Sergio Goic is certain to have gone to a good place up in the sky. Who could be so cruel? What did the clever man know that someone didn't want him to reveal?

Was the US or Russian military behind the ending of the Professor's life or was there another force at play?

Then there was the Adam Kennedy mystery. There was still no proof where and Adam disappeared or how he vanished. Likewise, there was no evidence to suggest that Adam was indeed dead.

Alan Falcon had let on that Adam knew about the legend that people of earth were meant to be a workforce of the gods.

Glory knew that Adam was no fool. Despite his age, he was an experienced archaeologist and he clearly knew much about the secret space program. He must have been on a mission to find something of such importance that it needed to go with him on the spaceship to safety before Planet Earth was destroyed by the mass destruction UFO called Planet X.

Glory thanked and paid the cab driver and went into the double story home. Rachel's face lit up as she saw her mother, while Adam Jnr was more interested in gulping down his supper. He finished the last of his baby food and let out a huge burp.

"Thanks, Adam," said his mother sarcastically.

"It is nice to see you too."

Glory spent some quality family time with the twins in order to give housekeeper a break.

Later, the ladies swapped roles and Glory made her way to the study room.

The razor-sharp former planetology student didn't know what she was looking for or where to start. She would only know when she saw it.

As she walked into the study, her eyes caught on the range of encyclopedia books that Adam had given to her as Christmas present. She pulled out some of the books and paged through each of them. They were all space-related and she had read them a few times.

Again, something caught her eye. On one of the pages was the number '1416'. She read the page carefully. At last! She had found a clue. The information on the page clearly stated that Planet Mars is roughly 1416 million miles away from Planet Earth!

Glory wiped her hands over her face. The first time that she had seen the numbers '1416', was on the message received to alert her of the disappearance of Adam Kennedy and the others on the mission with him.

Glory, you fool, she thought. That is it. Adam had put the numbers on the message as a code to tell her that he is still alive. She began to retrace her thoughts. Was she going crazy or was she making sense?

If Adam was indeed alive, why had he not made contact with her? Was he being held somewhere against his will and by whom: the US military, the Russian military or by a criminal force?

She could feel cold sweat dripping down her cheeks. Was her husband or the US government hiding something from her?

Glory Falcon moved over to her Celestron Powerseeker 70AZ Telescope which stood in the corner of the room near the window.

She began to adjust the telescopic settings like she did on many occasion, but this time, her fingers worked the switches on the device with aggression rather than finesse.

Glory peered into the eyepiece which would allow her to see out into space. There was something out there, there had to be!

She looked long and hard in an attempt to spot a UFO or perhaps, a US or Russian spaceship on its way to or back from Mars.

For afew seconds, everything looked normal through the telescope. Then, things changed for the worst. A blaze of light, similar to what Glory had seen through the telescope at the university and again on Prom Night, powered its way almost directly towards her telescope. For a moment, it seemed like the light was going to come right through the device. It was so bright that the mother of the twins pulled away and fell to the floor, letting out a loud cry.

The housekeeper, Joey Lawrence, found Glory Falcon lying motionless on the floor. She was conscious, but shivering from fear.

"Ms Glory, what happened?" asked a concerned Joey, as she tried to help her boss up to a seated position.

Glory tried to gather her thoughts.

"Joey, do you believe in Armageddon?" she asked.

The domestic worker reached for the sideboard and poured some water into a glass, before handing it to Glory.

"Yeah, I believe that the world will end someday and we will all be answerable to our maker on the way that we lived the life that he gave to us," said Joey.

Glory pushed in the next question.

"Joey, do you think that there are people living on other planets like Mars, Jupiter, and Uranus?"

Joey raised her eyebrows in surprise at the question.

"I am not sure if there are other humans living there. in fact, I don't think so, but there could well be other forms of life there," she said.

Glory took in a sip of water from the glass.

Suddenly, things were starting to make sense. If that bright light was able to strike at her through a telescope or without a telescope like on Prom Night, surely it could strike at other people too. Glory knew to always trust her gut feeling and it was telling her that the bright light may have blinded Professor Goic which forced him to lose control of his vehicle which then went over the cliff.

Her mind was in overdrive. Was a bright light from somewhere in the solar system also responsible for the potential death of Adam Kennedy? Was the bright light destroying anyone or anything that stood a chance of fighting against Planet X's chances of destroying everything on Planet Earth?

Was this a part of the secret project that the US and Russian military were fighting against? What was behind Planet X and what was the ultimate objective? Did Planet X have a Plan B to destroy anything that left Planet Earth? For instance, would Planet X have a means to destroy a spaceship en route from Earth to Mars?

She would only find the answers if she could work out the matters behind Planet X? How was it created and why of all the planets in the solar system, was it aimed at Planet Earth? Yes, earth was the only planet where humans were living to the best knowledge of the scientists, but who was on a mission to destroy what was now seen as a wicked 'workforce' for the gods?

Joey helped Glory to stand up from the floor. They went to the lounge, where Rachel and Adam Jnr were playing with toys peacefully on a woollen blanket.

The twins looked so peaceful and innocent, yet some force wanted to destroy all forms of life on earth – both good and bad.

Her thoughts were broken by the ringing of the doorbell.

Who would be coming to visit the Falcon home at this time of the evening?

Joey Lawrence went to answer the door and two men, one white and the other African-American, stood on the doorstep, both neatly dressed in black suits and wearing ties.

"Good evening, Ma'am, is this the Falcon residence," said the white man, who was slightly the thinner of the two.

Joey nodded, adding that this was the home of Mr and Mrs Alan Falcon.

The men waved their badges which identified them as FBI agents and Joey let them into the house and ushered them into the lounge.

"Mr Alan is not home yet," she said.

"We are not here to see Mr Falcon," explained the African-American agent, whose name was Denver Mills.

"We would like to speak with Mrs Falcon."

Glory had earlier retreated to the library room next to the lounge and eve-dropped on the conversation.

Back in the lounge, Joey offered the men tea or coffee but they both declined. They had both had a long working day and wanted to complete the reason for the call as quickly as possible so they could return to their respective families.

Glory made her way to the lounge and found one of the FBI men playing with one of Adam Jnr's toy cars in a bid to keep the child entertained. Adam roared with laughter as the FBI agent made a 'vroom, vroom' sound with his mouth as if to show him the sound that cars makes in reality.

Upon seeing Glory Falcon walk into the room, the FBI agent put the toy down and introduced himself and his colleague to the lady of the house.

"Good evening, Ma'am," said the thinner agent.

"We know that you are aware of the Project X threat and the US and Russian government's collaboration to space lift human life to Mars for safety reasons," he began.

Glory remained still and neither nodded nor spoke. Was Alan Falcon going to be court-marshalled for speaking to his wife about sensitive secret projects?

"Well, we are not here to take action against you or your husband," the agent went on.

"We actually need your help."

Glory gulped. Of what benefit could she actually be to the FBI?

"Ma'am, you used to be involved in a relationship with Adam Kennedy, am I correct?' the agent said.

This time Glory had no option but to nod in agreement.

"Ms Falcon, we need to find Adam Kennedy as he could be an important part of what is going to happen in the bigger scheme of things. You need to be open and honest with us. Do you know where Adam is?"

Glory was taken aback. Surely she should be the one asking the FBI men if they knew where Adam Kennedy is?

Glory tried to speak but no words came out.

The bigger of the two agents could see that the woman was in complete shock.

"Ms Falcon, what do you know about a bright light from the solar system?"

Again, Glory stared on. How did the bright light link in with the disappearance of Adam?

"Ma'am, Adam Kennedy went in search of a very important item in the Amazon which is a key link to the bright light and the Project X problem."

Glory shook her head. It was as if the FBI men were speaking in riddles. How could the bright light be linked to a treasured item that Adam had been searching for in the Amazon? She felt like she was building a puzzle in her mind but most of the pieces were lying on the floor rather than on the table in front of her.

"Ma'am the bright light that you have witnessed is reflecting off of the item that Mr Kennedy was searching for and anyone who comes in contact with the glares could face instant death," said the African-American FBI man.

"A Professor in Chile has already been killed in this manner."

Ah, so she was right about how Professor Goic met his maker, thought Glory

"Then why am I still alive after being struck three times by the blinding light? asked Glory.

"That is exactly what we want to know from you," asked the thinner agent in a stern tone.

"What is your link to the 'Corridor'?"

Chapter Eight

Safety comes first

The silence was deafening inside the Oval office as US President John Carmichael III sat staring at the 'three wise men' seated in front of him.

Dressed in a grey suit, and wearing a white shirt and yellow, black-striped tie, the American No 1 had done well in his first year in the White House. Some would not attest to that fact. He was like the average company CEO. He thought things through hundreds of time before making a decision rather than relying on gut feeling and common sense. Then again, if you are responsible for the lives of over 323 million people, he really had little option other than to think of it in that fashion.

Something needed to happen that can break icy tension in the room. The President began to tap his US$1800 Conway Stewart Teal Fountain Pen against his notepad.

Chief of Security, Myles Jenkins, puffed out his cheeks. Economics advisor, Stan Appelby, sat staring at the floor, shaking his head. Space program advisor, Shaun Kelly, was staring at his Tablet computer, wiping his forehead with his handkerchief on few occasions, more out of stress than sweat running down his face.

"How much time have we got?" asked President Carmichael.

Shaun looked up from his Tablet computer.

"It is very hard to tell, sir," he replied.

"It could be today, it could be tomorrow, it could be next month or next year. Planet X seems to adjust its speed continuously. The navigational symptoms all shows that it is heading for Planet Earth, but it was moving much faster a week ago than how it has over the past two days.

The President continued to throw questions at his advisors.

"How safe are out spaceships and how many people can we evacuate at a time? How many spaceships do we have available?"

Again Shaun piped up.

"Sir, each spaceship can accommodate around one thousand people including staffs," he answered.

"We have one hundred of these vehicles and two hundred and fifty if we include the Russian spaceships."

President Carmichael's head jolted backwards. He was a firm believer that the Russians could not be trusted in any situation. Weren't they the ones who had helped former President Donald Trump rig the election through email hacking, so that he would get into power ahead of Democratic candidate Hillary Clinton?

"How safe are those Russian spaceships if we are going to put American lives onboard of them?" asked the President, looking at Myles Jenkins.

Jenkins, who had worked in the White House for the past thirty years knew his President's emotional habits better than anyone. He was almost hesitant to answer the question. Myles knew that President Carmichael listened to the first sentence of what anyone told him and would only listen more if he liked what he was hearing. If not, he switched his mind off of the subject.

"Sir, the Russian spaceships could well be safer than our own," commented the Chief of Security.

"With due respect, the Russians spent over ten times more on their own space program over the past ten years compared to our budget."

President Carmichael stood up from his chair and began to pace up and down the room, staring out of the Oval Office window from time to time.

Stan Appelby, the President's leading bean counter in terms of the US Dollar, could read the mind of his leader.

"Sir, we have an extra twenty billion available to throw at this project, you know that."

The President turned around at speed. He didn't like being reminded of such things for one simple reason. He had no time for the space program. He didn't believe in it, let alone throw billions of taxpayers' cash at it. John Carmichael III lived in a world of his own. The space program was nothing more than a figment of someone's imagination, according to him.

How on earth could the lives of people on our own planet be in danger by something called Planet X? He didn't believe in UFOs. President Carmichael thought that UFOs were only spotted by people who had too much to drink. What would be next; Little green aliens landing from Mars at John F Kennedy International Airport? No. He would be tar and feathered if he threw twenty billion US Dollars at this pie-in-the-sky campaign.

"Time is ticking, sir. We can't take the risk of leaving things too late," said Shaun.

"It's not about our lives. We have all experienced life to a degree. It's about the future generations of America."

President Carmichael's eyes were raging in the direction of Shaun. He didn't respond with his thoughts, but what was going through his mind was: 'you mean the future generations of Mars citizens, Shaun, because that is what they will be'.

President Carmichael's drifted from the face of Shaun to Myles and then Stan. Would these well-educated and experienced men really consider sending American citizens to outer space forever? Or was it a case of the President of the US who was out of touch with reality and who should use his expensive fountain pen to sign a letter of resignation as leader of one of the most powerful nations on earth?

"Perhaps we should have a meeting with the Russians or a Skype chat at least?" he asked.

The last thing that the US No 1 wanted at this point was to spend quality time chatting with his Russian counterpart, but it seemed like he has no other option. Former President Trump had created a channel of communication with the Russians which many of his predecessors were against.

The desk phone next to the President's notepad sprung to life with a buzzing sound and was answered by the country's leading politician.

"Sir, US Head of Military Operations, Ted Kingsley is on the line for you, may I put the call through?" asked the White House secretary Gillian Kent over the phone.

The call was put through and President Carmichael began to chat with the military head. Those in the room could sense that there was a good relationship between the two men. After all, any leader of a nation would know to keep his military man close. If ever a President was to be unseated by a coup de'tat overthrow.

An example of this was recently seen in southern Africa where Zimbabwe's ruthless Robert Mugabe had his dictatorial, 37 years of leadership ended by being overthrown by his own military.

"Ted, what's happening?" asked the President to his military chief.

"John, the North Koreans are one step away from blowing Guam out of the water," said the frustrated and tense military boss.

The tensions between North Korea and the US had reached fever pitch a few months earlier when the North Korean President, Kin Jong Un, had threatened to launch a full-scale nuclear attack on the US territory island of Guam if then-President Trump did not refrain from his threat of disarming the North Korean nuclear program by force.

President Carmichael was fully aware of the Guam/North Korea problem. He had hoped that the issue would disappear now that former President Trump had left the White House.

"What has brought about Kim's reincarnation of the threats on Guam?" asked the President.

Ted Kingsley responded.

"Kim has heard that the US is working closely with the Russians on a space program, which he sees as a means for the US to heavily arm military equipment. Kim doesn't believe the spaceship story. He thinks that the US and Russians are working together to have a full go at North Korea to disarm their nuclear program."

President Carmichael shook his head. First, he had his 'three wise men' telling him that Americans should live out their lives in Mars and now he had the North Koreans threatening to blow an island full of Americans off the face of the earth. This just further enhanced the President's view that the 'Corridor' project was actually more trouble than it was worth.

The President thanked Ted Kingsley for the heads-up and asked his secretary to send Press Secretary, Peter Cox, to the Oval Office.

A minute later, Peter Cox, a man in his forties dressed in a black suit with a matching tie, arrived. He greeted the President and 'the three wise men'.

For the next thirty minutes, those in the Oval Office discussed the pros and cons of the situation. The space program between the Russians and the Americans was supposed to have been a secret one. However, if the North Korean government opened their mouths about it in the media, then it won't be much of a secret after all, will it?

Should the Americans go with a media statement? Would it be better to have the public informed by their leader, the American President, rather than reading about the North Korean President's quotes in a newspaper or television interview?

"President, sir, you have to push the button before it is too late," said Shaun Kelly, in reference to the transportation of Americans by spaceship to Mars.

"Surely the North Koreans military will know the difference between a spaceship on its way to Mars and a spaceship sent in their direction?"

President Carmichael's fear was that the moment the first spaceship was launched from Cape Canaveral, the first nuclear weapon could be sent towards Guam. John Carmichael III made the point that the North Koreans operated on a 'do it now and think later' approach rather than the other way around.

"How safe is this 'Corridor'?" asked President Carmichael.

"I mean, if a spaceship is sent to orbit, surely the North Korean nuclear weapons won't reach it there?"

The 'three wise men' agreed. The North Korean nuclear weapons were not designed to destroy objects in outer space.

That left the Guam issue? The Americans could not take the risk of emptying the islands of all life forms. The North Koreans would surely smell a rat and could quite easily take aim at another US-occupied island or other land-space.'

The citizens of Guam, the island in the Pacific Ocean, are known as Guamanians and are American citizens by birth.

"Sir," remarked Shaun Kelly.

"I have read an interesting story about an American planetology graduate from the University of Chicago who may know more about this. Apparently, she was dating an archaeologist who disappeared in the Amazon while searching for an artifact that is key to this whole story."

The President gazed at Shaun.

"Where is this woman now?" asked the President.

"I believe that FBI agents have been sent to interrogate her," replied Shaun.

"I have also read that she recently married physicist, Alan Falcon, who is a senior operations man on the space program at Cape Canaveral."

Shaun passed the print out of the page to the President, whose eyes were caught on the beauty of Glory Falcon.

"Tell the agents to bring her to the White House," quipped the American No 1.

Shaun Kelly left the room to relay the President's orders to the FBI office down the passage.

President Carmichael placed his hands over his face. If it wasn't Planet X trying to blow them away, then it was the North Koreans. He had often heard the slogan of 'tough at the top but crowded at the bottom'. Right now, he wishes that he was at the bottom and not the world's leading politician.

He had always wanted to be a politician and the Pussycat Dolls hit song played on his mind, 'Be careful what you wish for cuz you just might get it' was racing through his mind.

With the news about a potential North Korean onslaught on Guam, the 'Corridor' project was becoming more and more of a solution in the mind of President Carmichael. Unbeknown to the others in the room, he was now just a step away from spending that extra twenty billion in cash on the project.

He could envisage himself strapped in on a spaceship with his family en route to Mars. Goodness knows that this planet could only be a better and safer place than earth at the moment.

Chapter Nine

White House, here I come

Back at the Falcon home at Cocoa Beach, a match was taking place. It wasn't football, tennis or any other sport, but rather a shouting match.

"I am telling you for the last time, I don't know where Adam Kennedy is and I know nothing about the artifact that he was searching for in the Amazon," said a distraught Glory Falcon, who was being interrogated in the comfort of her lounge by FBI agents, Dirk Lange and Scott Rogers.

Neither was buying into Glory's innocence.

"Ms Falcon, don't play the innocent game with us," said the thin white agent, Dirk Lange, in a stern voice.

"We have brought down large crime syndicates who also protested that they know nothing. In fact, word is that we are able to make the deaf talk if you know what I mean?"

Glory gulped. She was pretty sure that neither agent would lay a hand on her.

"Do you want to know what I think, Ms Falcon?" questioned Scott Rogers.

"I think that you are a two-timing gold-digging little cow. You knew exactly where Adam Kennedy was headed to in order to collect the treasured item and when he didn't return with it which would have changed your life financially, you went the other way. Wow, Ms Falcon, this mansion that you stay in must be worth quite a bit?"

Glory burst into tears.

"It is not what you think," she said in a sobbing tone.

"I am not like that at all. It isn't like that at all."

Agent Rogers continued.

"Then you had better tell us what you know or else we have no option but to conclude what I have just stated."

Glory ran her hands over her face to push her black hair out of the way.

"Somebody booked Adam at short notice for the Amazon mission," she said.

"He left on Christmas Day. He wouldn't tell me what he was looking for or who booked the mission. You know how it is? You can't tell your family members half the stuff that you do or see in your daily jobs. It's simply too dangerous."

Agent Dirk Lange wasn't convinced.

"Tell us about your phone call to the Paranal Observatory in Chile?"

Again Glory gulped.

How did the FBI know about her chat with the assistant to the late Professor Goic? Was her mobile phone and home phone tapped by the government agency? Did they know about the bright light that had thrown her to the floor at the University of Chicago's laboratory, as well as at Prom Night and upstairs in her home here at Cocoa Beach?

Did the FBI also think that the bright light from outer space, quite possibly from Planet X, had also blinded Professor Goic so much that he had lost control of his car before going over the cliff?

Glory had so many questions racing through her mind, but she needed to tread carefully as she wasn't sure what the FBI men did or did not know.

Agent Dirk Lange spoke again.

"We believe that you were trying to make contact with Professor Goic at the Paranal Observatory because you had some important information to pass on to him about the space program and you knew that he had been working on it for quite some years via a powerful telescope."

"You know by now that Professor Goic is deceased. His car went over the cliff. We don't believe that there was foul play involved but did find something strange on his body."

Glory Falcon listed carefully.

"There was a burn mark, about three square inches on his right arm," went on Agent Lange.

"It was almost as if a UFO had launched a ray from outer space to take him out."

Glory ran her left arm up her right with the aim of reaching her shoulder, but it didn't get that far. She felt a large bump, pretty close to a type of mark near where her right arm joined the body. She couldn't remember it being there before. She tried to rub the mark without making it too obvious to the FBI men.

The bright light that had stunned her and burnt the Professor before he drove his car over the edge, had clearly been on a mission to end her life too, on no fewer than three occasions.

Agent Dirk Lange stood up from his seat near the lounge window. The curtains had not yet been drawn although it was well past dusk.

"Ms Falcon, we don't know what your husband is telling our other FBI team at the space office, but my friend out there, Agent Scott Rogers, is not a man known for having much patience and he is close to reaching his limit with you."

Glory stared at the African-American and he stared back at her with a fierce look on his face.

"However, we are honourable gentlemen, so we are giving you one hour to reconsider your story," said Agent Lange.

"You can speak to whoever you like, but I would be careful on that front if I were you. We will return in an hour. To hear what you have decided to tell us. Oh, don't even think of making a run for it. That would definitely not be in your best interest."

The agents headed towards the front door of the Falcon mansion and let themselves out.

Glory did not move an inch from her seat on the sofa near the fireplace.

What had Adam Kennedy got her into? She lived a happy family life and now America's most senior law enforcers were accusing her of withholding information that could put the safety of the nation in jeopardy.

Adam, where are you, she thought.

However, back at the space station, things weren't going too well for Alan Falcon either. He was an innocent man but the FBI agents there were beginning to think differently.

Nice guys finish last, so the saying goes...

....

Alan Falcon's hope of an early night home to spend time with his family was straight out the window. Two FBI men, built like the guys you see in action in Wrestlemania on television, had come to visit him.

"Look here, Falcon, I am not sure what game you are playing but you are putting the security of over 300 million people at risk," said FBI Agent Stuart Williams.

"You have special clearance to most areas of the space program but it's the data that we are worried about.

Alan did not understand and requested more information.

Agent Keith Rundle was happy to oblige.

"How can Planet X move at 800 miles per hour on one day and only 300 the next? This information impacts on how soon Planet X will arrive on earth or more specifically, how much time we have at our disposal to evacuate earth."

Alan was also at his wit's end to answer the question that had just been posed to him.

As a physicist, it was also quite intriguing to him as far as Planet X's change in speed was concerned. There was absolutely no consistency about it.

"Well Falcon, I can tell you that the distance issue has reached as high a level as the desk of US President John Carmichael III since he needs to know exactly how to handle the situation and how much time we have at our disposal," said Agent Williams.

Alan shook his head.

"Gentlemen, I am just as puzzled about the speed or lack of it, as you and the President is," said the physicist.

"It is almost like someone is with a remote controlling it from Planet Earth."

The two agents stared at Alan.

"Oh no, come on guys," said Alan.

"You surely don't think that I am playing a part in remote controlling Planet X from my office desk? I mean that is absurd. I am a family man. I mean what would be in it for me to derail or speed up the process?"

Agent Keith Rundle was happy to give his view some thoughts.

"Well, if you sped up the process, you would make more money. As you always say: 'Nothing personal, it's purely business, gentlemen'."

Before Alan could reply, Stuart Williams took over.

"So then what do you know about the sudden disappearance of Adam Kennedy, the archaeologist extraordinaire fame?"

Alan dared not look away from Stuart Williams for fear of being told that he is guilty of withholding information. The FBI men knew how to analyze body language. You had to have some sort of psychology understanding to work in the field for the FBI, Alan had always thought.

"I know nothing about the disappearance of Adam Kennedy," answered Alan with a sense of confidence.

Keith Rundle giggled.

"It was quite convenient that Kennedy disappears and you marry the love of his life in almost no time at all."

Alan Falcon had a Parker ballpoint pen in his hand. For a moment, he thought about throwing the pen with much force in the direction of the FBI man, but fortunately, common sense prevailed.

"Why the sudden interest in the space program anyway?" he asked.

"I mean the US President has shown no interest in it since he came to power just over a year ago. The program is getting a few pennies compared with other projects in the budget at the White House."

Keith Rundle adjusted his black tie and began to explain.

"That is where you are wrong, Falcon," he said.

"The US President has signed orders to make US$20 billion available for the construction of as many spaceships as possible over the next ninety days. That is if you can give your word that Planet X won't come crashing into us before the ninety days is up."

Alan Falcon nearly fell off his chair. Why the sudden change of heart from the No 1 in the Oval Office?

The physicist was no fool. He worked out rather quickly that another country may have threatened war against the US and he wouldn't be surprised if it was the North Koreans with their strong nuclear weaponry.

"Gentlemen, I will re-check and double-check the data regarding Planet X again, but for some reason, it gives me irregular figures everytime I check it," said Alan.

"I am not playing a game here. I get paid to transport human lives to a safer place like Mars and believe me, that is exactly what I intend to do as quickly as possible."

For a moment, it looked like the FBI men believed him. He had a day from hell at the office and convincing law enforcers was just the cherry on top. What could possibly make the day any worse: Perhaps, Adam Kennedy walking through his office door?

Whether the FBI men wanted to believe him or not, he didn't know where Adam Kennedy was, nor did he have all the facts about the artifact that Adam had been chasing.

If anybody knew the answers, it would be Glory, but he believed her when she said that Adam was very secretive about his mission on Christmas Eve prior to his departure.

"If I were you, I would get on the phone and make a call to Moscow, because time is ticking," said Stuart Williams to Alan.

"Have the FBI spoken to my wife?" asked the physicist.

Keith Rundle nodded.

"She is in good hands, don't you worry. Pretty little thing, isn't she?"

Alan Falcon gritted his teeth. He waited for the two FBI to leave his office and then checked his Planet X data again. Something was wrong. The UFO was supposed to be heading for Planet Earth at great speed, but yet, it was moving slower than yesterday or the past three days, as a matter of fact.

How was he supposed to make money and convince the White House and the Russians of this immense threat to human life when the threat was going slower and slower?

Was Armageddon a figment of his imagination?

Chapter Ten

Armageddon's too close

Glory Falcon wiped the tears from her eyes as she sat on the sofa in the lounge. Eventually, she lost control of her emotions and sobbed loudly. She had gone from an A-standard graduate to a criminal in the eyes of her government – a criminal who was putting the safety of all American citizens at risk.

Housekeeper, Joey Lawrence, heard the cries from her boss and ran down the passage to the lounge.

She put her right arm around the shoulders of Glory.

"Ms Glory, what is it?" she questioned.

Glory looked up into the eyes of the housekeeper. Why wasn't her life as simple as that of the 56-year-old woman, who at the tender age of two, had accompanied her parents to the US from Puerto Rico.

Nowadays, she was as much a US citizen as Glory was.

Joey had two wonderful kids, both with university degrees courtesy of scholarships that had followed their superb points at government schools.

Glory was adamant that Joey had problems in life to overcome as well, but she never aired them publicly. Even in tough times, Joey always had a smile on her face. She was a regular church-goer and ran her life by using the F-words; Faith and Forgiveness.

"How can you always see the brighter side of life when it isn't there, Joey?" asked Glory.

Joey pushed her greying medium length black hair away from her face and used an elastic band to tie it behind her head into a ponytail.

"My God always looks after my family, Ms Glory," she said with a little smile.

Glory bit her bottom lip as she thought.

"Joey, do you believe in Armageddon? I mean, do you believe that the world will end one day and only those who have lived by the Word of the Lord will make it into heaven?'

Joey nodded.

"My God forgives those who want to be forgiven, and yes, I do believe that the world will end one day, and the Son of God will return to earth right at the end."

Then two things happened. Adam Jnr and Rachel began to cry simultaneously. As Joey stood up to go and attend to them, the door-bell also rang and Glory told her that she would check who was at the door.

She looked at the grandfather clock in the corner of the lounge. It was 19h45. The FBI agents had left the property at 19h10 and had promised to give her an hour to gather her thoughts. Surely, the American law enforcement men were not back yet? She knew it couldn't possibly be Alan Falcon at the door. Firstly, he had a key to unlock the door and secondly, she knew that he was being interrogated by the FBI heavyweights at his office at Cape Canaveral.

She headed to the door in a huff almost certain to find FBI Agents Dirk Lange and Scott Rogers on her porch.

She opened the door and spoke before seeing the person or persons present.

"Agents Lange and Rogers, you said that I have one hour to gather my thoughts and…"

Glory Falcon stopped in mid-sentence as she recognized the individual standing just less than thirty inches from her face.

Glory's legs battled to support her upper body frame as she gazed into the eyes of the father of her twins. She just stared at Adam Kennedy for what in her mind seemed to be minutes or hours, but in reality was just a few seconds.

"Can I come inside or are you going to stare at me until Armageddon?"

"Yeah, Adam, please come inside. The FBI are swarming around Cape Canaveral and here asking about you and the artifact that you were pursuing," said Glory, as she ushered her visitor into the house and peered up and down the street to make sure that they weren't being watched, before shutting the front door.

As Adam walked into the lounge, his eyes caught on the wedding photograph of Alan Falcon and Glory, which was positioned in a small frame on the sideboard. Next, he saw the framed photographs of Adam Jnr and Rachel. The archaeologist was no fool. He could see his own eyes when he looked at the photographs of the twins.

"How old are they now?" he asked.

"Adam, I wanted to tell you but I had no way of making contact," said a distraught Glory, who could see how much Adam Kennedy was hurting.

"Glory, I have so much to tell you," said Adam, dressed in a smart tweed overcoat and black pants. Glory gazed at her ex-lover. He looked even more handsome now than when he had left for the Amazon mission. His facial features were far more positive than what she had witnessed on the last video message that had been sent to her Tablet computer.

"Adam, I have so many questions for you too," she quipped.

"Tell me about the artifact, Adam. The FBI will be here any minute looking for you and the artifact. They think that I know your whereabouts and hiding information from them. They believe that because of the artifact which is coupled to the space program, I am placing the lives of millions of American citizens at risk."

Glory continued.

"The other FBI team is busy interrogating Alan Falcon as we speak. Armageddon is getting closer and if the space program doesn't get activated soon, all aspects of human life are at risk. Tell me what is going on, Adam. Please tell me."

Glory sat on the sofa opposite Adam and was feeling so weak. In fact, she felt weaker than when she was struggling to stand upright when she had answered the front door a few minutes earlier. It was like the world was coming to an end for Glory Falcon, if not for all human life on the planet, then just for Glory Falcon. Armageddon's too close.

Adam Kennedy licked his lips. He could see the emotional pain stretched across Glory's face. What wouldn't he give just to hold her tight and kiss her. Alas, she was no longer his woman. Alan Falcon had married her while he had been missing on the Amazon mission. Adam Kennedy had no problem with Alan. The men had never been friends but respected each other's abilities in their respective fields of expertise.

Adam stared into Glory's eyes. The love chemistry was still there.

Eventually, Glory looked away.

"Adam, it's too late for anything to happen between us now," she said.

"Time has marched on. Fate stepped in to keep us apart. I am married. Let's just accept it for what it is."

But just when she decided to stop loving Adam and be a good wife to Alan, when she vowed not to let Adam sneak into her mind again, she met Adam again by accident or fate, she couldn't tell.

Adam Kennedy was about to respond when the doorbell rang again. This time, Glory was adamant that the FBI agents were back and standing on her front porch.

"My God, Adam, quick, hide in the pantry cupboard just off the kitchen," she said.

"These FBI guys don't play around."

Adam ran out of the lounge and Glory could hear his shoes rubbing against the wooden floorboards until it eventually reached silence.

"Glory made her way to the front door. She was very sure of what she was going to tell the FBI agents. Fortunately, she didn't have too.

"Good evening, again, Agent Lange and Rogers," she said, as she greeted the law enforcers and ushered them into the lounge.

"You struck it lucky, didn't you?" questioned Dirk Lange.

"What do you mean?" asked Glory.

"We have received orders from the Oval Office to transport you there with immediate effect," said Scott Rogers.

Glory swallowed hard.

"The Oval Office… That is the No 1's office."

"Yeah, the orders to transport you there came directly from the office of US President John Carmichael III," commented Scott.

Dirk Lange moved over to the lounge window and out of routine, lifted the curtain to make sure that there was nobody listening to their conversation. "Ms Falcon, while you are packing an overnight bag of clothes of toiletries, you don't mind if we checked the house?" he asked.

"I mean we would hate to have been here for a few hours only to find out afterwards that Adam Kennedy is hiding in your fridge," he joked.

Glory produced a forced laugh. If only the agent knew how close he was to the truth. She said a little silent prayer for Adam, hoping that the powers above would protect him.

"Sure, by all means, have a look around," responded Glory.

Agent Scott Rogers turned to his colleague, Dirk Lange.

"Let me check upstairs, you check downstairs."

Dirk agreed and soon the FBI men were walking through the house checking cupboards and any other potential hiding places.

Dirk checked some of the downstairs' rooms and eventually made his way to the kitchen.

Please, Lord. Glory thought to herself. About three minutes went by before Dirk returned to the lounge.

Scott Rogers joined him there a few minute later.

"All clean on my side. Agent Lange, what about you?" asked the African-American agent.

"Clean as a whistle on my side too," remarked Dirk.

Glory was upstairs packing her overnight bag, but the agents were speaking loud enough for her to hear everything.

Glory didn't know exactly where Adam was until she heard a slight whistle from near her bedroom window. She glanced outside and there was Adam Kennedy, gripping for dear life onto the stairs of the porch railings. Adam winked at her as if to say send regards to the US No 1.

Glory blew a kiss to him and shut the curtains. At least she knew that Adam was safe. So was his artifact and its secret. After-all, she didn't have a chance to discuss it with him, let alone the FBI agents.

"Ms Falcon, we really have to go now," bellowed Agent Dirk Lange from downstairs.

"We will travel via helicopter to the mainland and climb on an aircraft to take us to Washington D.C."

Glory gave Joey a hug. She knew that her twins were in good hands."

Wow, she thought, little Glory Falcon on her way to meet with the US President! Who would ever have thought?

The FBI agents walked Glory to a yellow Ford Mustang vehicle parked at the front of the property.

Dirk Lange opened the rear door for her to climb in and shut it after her, while Scott Rogers placed Glory's luggage in the boot.

As the vehicle pulled off from its parked position, she looked back at the Falcon home. Did she hope to see Adam Kennedy waving at her? No, she wanted one final look as she wasn't sure if she would ever see the mansion again. Planet X was her enemy, not the FBI.

Another few minutes passed and before she knew it, Glory was air bound inside a military helicopter that was taking her to the mainland.

She looked out of the window and what she saw was darkness, which reminded her of her endless hours of staring out into space through the various telescopes that she had worked with.

How far off was Armageddon? How safe were the spaceships? Could the US military trust their Russian counterparts? How safe was the 'Corridor'?

Like Glory and Adam had said earlier to each other, there were so many unanswered questions. How Glory wished that the US President would be able to answer some of them, but her gut feeling told her otherwise. It seemed that the US President wanted answers from her.

As for Adam Kennedy – initially he was her saviour and lover and now he was in her past, but she still had his back. Between Adam, Alan, and Glory, they held the keys to the 'Corridor' more than the US or Russian military ever would.

Glory Falcon again glanced out of the helicopter window into the darkness. The darkness seemed to be a part of her life, except for that blinding light!

She hadn't experienced it for a while: would it come back to haunt her? Was her destiny within the 'Corridor'?

TO BE CONTINUED

STRONGHOLDS part NOW

X-RAY DAYS part AFTER

88735555R00083

Made in the USA
Columbia, SC
03 February 2018